That One Spooky Night

Written by Dan Bar-el
Illustrated by David Huyck

Kids Can Press

SOME SAY IT WAS THE PLANETS' DOING.

SOME SAY IT WAS ALL JUST A BAD DREAM.

SOME SAY IT WAS AN EVIL WIZARD'S PLOT.

ACTUALLY, ONLY ONE SAID THAT.

THAT ONE *SPOOKY NIGHT.*

7

9

14

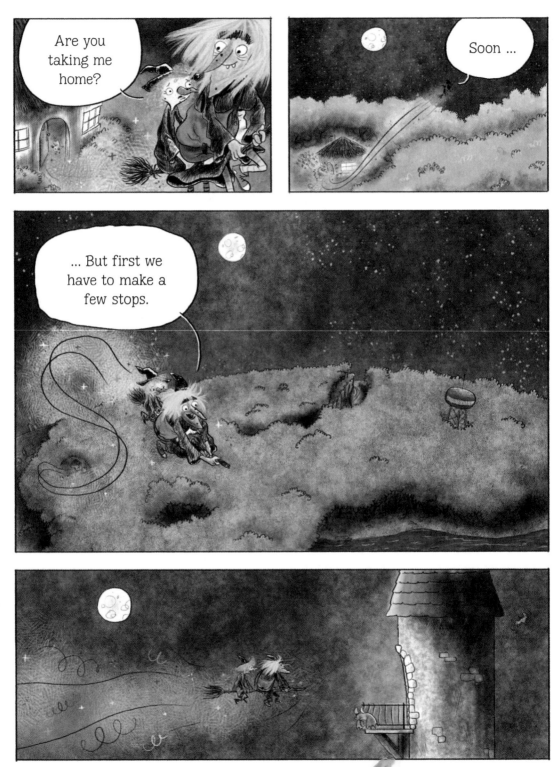

I'll just leave it here, Trollie.
I know you're hungry.

Eat up, everyone.
You're looking
awfully skinny.

Dad would like to
go home now.

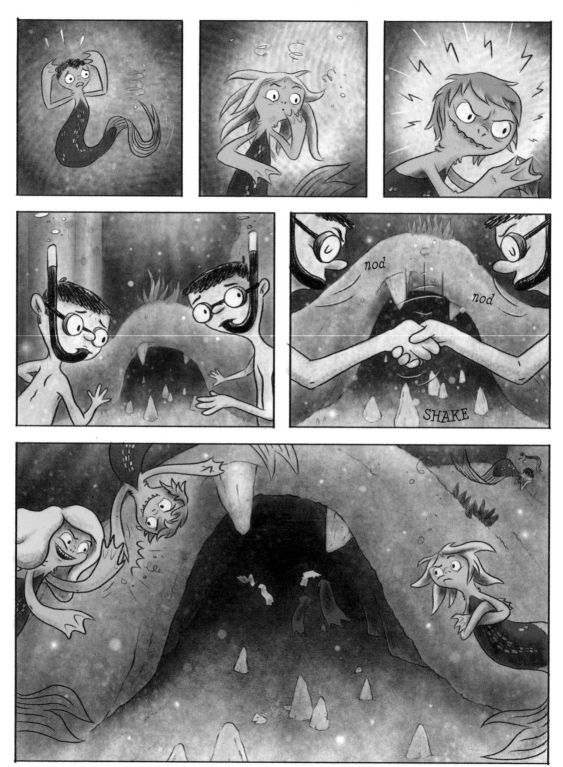

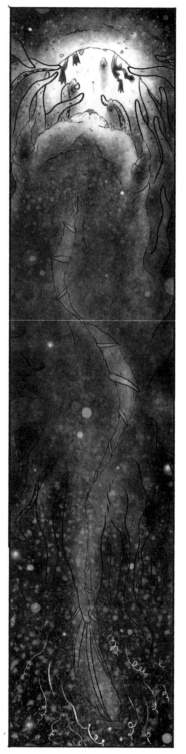

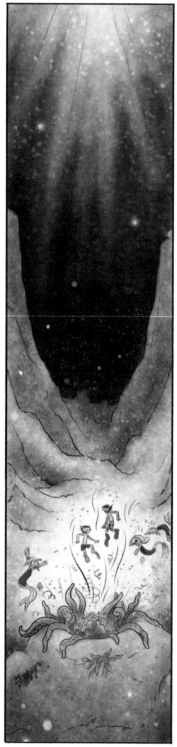

pant
pant
pant

PHOO

ZZZ ...

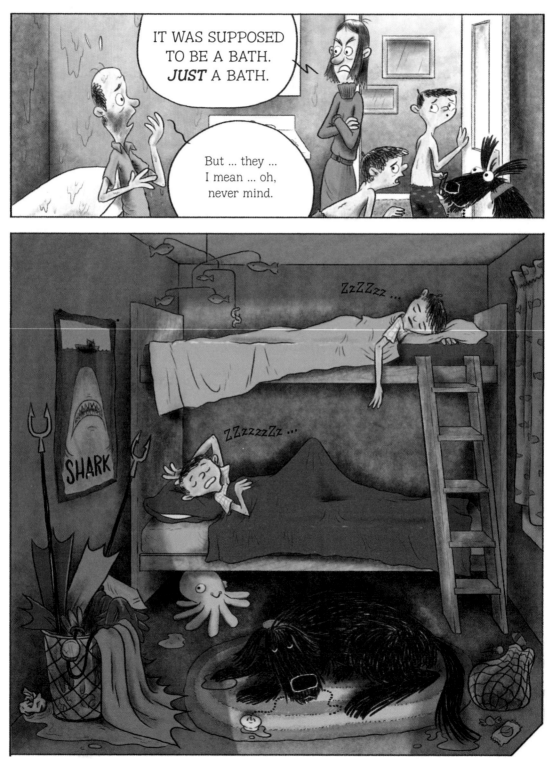

A *NURSE*? A *FAIRY*? GIVE ME A **BREAK!**

A BALLERINA AND A MERMAID? *THAT IS SO LAME!*

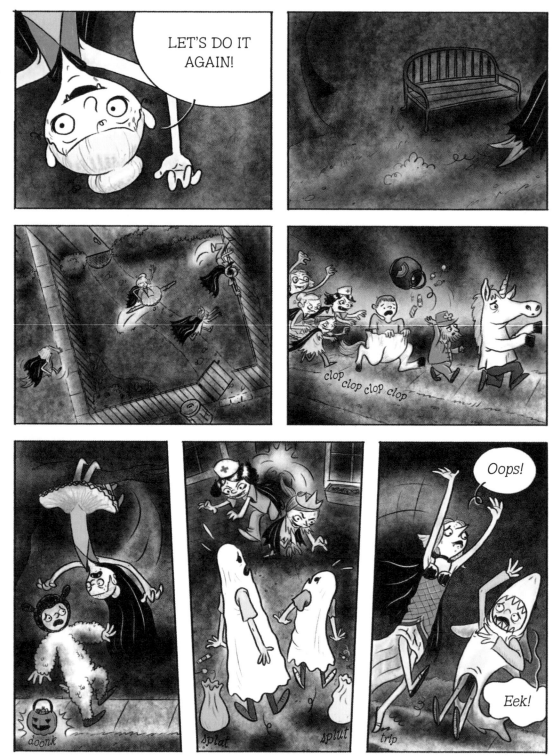

EWWW, GROSS!

THAT LAST KID WAS *TOO* SCARED.

HEY, LOOK! IT'S THOSE BOYS WHO CALLED US *LAME.*

What **dingbat** is trying to say is that we live there, next door, and we're having a party. *Wanna come?*

A **HALLOWEEN** PARTY? WITH FOOD AND DRINKS?

YEAH, SURE, A *HALLOWEEN* PARTY.

With **LOTS** of drinks. *HEH HEH HEH.*

I don't remember ever seeing this place before.

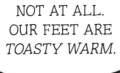

AWESOME DECORATIONS!

THE PARTY IS IN HERE!

THIS ISN'T A *PARTY!* THERE'S NO *MUSIC.* THERE'S *NO FOOD.* THERE'S *NOTHING* TO DRINK!

THE DOOR WON'T **OPEN!**

I'M SURE YOUR PARENTS VOULD NOT BE PLEASED. NEXT TIME CALL FIRST TO MAKE A *PLAY DATE.*

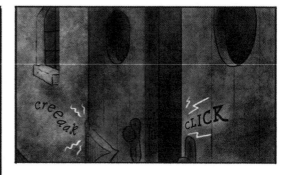

creeaak

CLICK

I had fun tonight. Let's do this again!

...GHT ...

BUT NOT JUST ANY NIGHT ...

GRRRRRR

ARROOOo

ARROOOo

SOMETHING HAPPENED.

Hoo!
HOO!

IT HAPPENED HERE ...

THAT ONE *SPOOKY NIGHT.*

For Dad, who once made me the coolest astronaut costume ever — D.B.
Thank you forever to Cailin. For my little monsters, Susanna and Oscar — D.H.

Text © 2012 Dan Bar-el
Illustrations © 2012 David Huyck

Kids Can Press acknowledges the financial support of the Government of Ontario, through the Ontario Media Development Corporation's Ontario Book Initiative; the Ontario Arts Council; the Canada Council for the Arts; and the Government of Canada, through the BPIDP, for our publishing activity.

Published in Canada by
Kids Can Press Ltd.
25 Dockside Drive
Toronto, ON M5A 0B5

Published in the U.S. by
Kids Can Press Ltd.
2250 Military Road
Tonawanda, NY 14150

www.kidscanpress.com

Edited by Tara Walker and Karen Li
Designed by David Huyck and Rachel Di Salle

The hardcover edition of this book is smyth sewn casebound.
The paperback edition of this book is limp sewn with a drawn-on cover.
Manufactured in Shen Zhen, Guang Dong, P.R. China, in 5/2012 by Printplus Limited

CM 12 0 9 8 7 6 5 4 3 2 1
CM PA 12 0 9 8 7 6 5 4 3 2 1

Library and Archives Canada Cataloguing in Publication

Bar-el, Dan
      That one spooky night / written by Dan Bar-el ; illustrated by David Huyck.

ISBN 978-1-55453-751-8 (bound) ISBN 978-1-55453-752-5 (pbk.)

1. Graphic novels. I. Huyck, David, 1976– II. Title.

PN6733.B37T43 2012   j741.5'971   C2012-901589-X

Kids Can Press is a **(OrUS** Entertainment company